When Everything Changed: A Story of Montana Territory

By Tom Keith

Dedicated to the Keiths who made their way from New Brunswick to Montana Territory in the 1880s

*What is life? It is the flash of a firefly
in the night. It is the breath of a
buffalo in the wintertime. It is the little
shadow which runs across the grass
and loses itself in the sunset.*

—Crowfoot, Blackfoot ca 1830-1890

I.

In the early summer of 1882, the steamboat *Red Cloud*
slowly beat its way up the Missouri River, nearly two
months into a journey that had begun in St. Louis. On a
flawless day full of the promise of June, Daniel McHarg
stood on a deck piled high with wood and other clutter,
idly leaning against the rail, mesmerized by the play of
water against the hull. Where Daniel stood, the only
sound was the steady slapping of the paddle wheel, a
sound that had faded into the background after several
weeks of travel.

In his relaxed state, Daniel was startled when a few
buffalo appeared, swimming toward the boat, their
great collective bulk appearing like a small moving
island. As the distance between the buffalo and the
boat closed, a rifle shot, followed by several more, rang
out from the deck above. One of the shooter's targets
was a cow that swam with her two calves. The shots
seemed to have no effect initially, but as the boat
approached the beast stopped lateral movement and
began a slow drift downriver. She passed close to
where Daniel stood, her life reduced to a few last
twitches, the blood flowing through her nostrils adding
its color to the already dark water.

Daniel watched the carcass drift until a scuffle on the upper deck grabbed his attention. The *Red Cloud's* captain, a thick man with powerful hands, had one of the passengers in his grip. After several weeks of travel on the confined spaces of the boat, the captain had shown himself to be a calm man, but now his blood was up. He jerked the rifle from the shooter and hurled it into the river, his powerful voice carrying to where Daniel stood well below:

"By God, if another fool tries this, I'll throw his ass overboard and keep the rifle!"

The captain immediately apologized for his language to the several women standing nearby but continued to handle the shooter roughly. Only with difficulty was he able to restrain himself from seriously hurting the man. The captain didn't give a damn about the buffalo; his concern was the safety of his passengers. He had decreed to all onboard that shooting would be allowed only from the lower deck, a commitment he had made after a similar incident had maimed a child on one of his trips downriver. He had vowed to never let it happen again. The shooter, whose clothes marked him as a city man, walked away shakily, showing the good sense not to make a fuss about his rough treatment or the loss of his rifle.

After the captain returned to the pilothouse, most of the passengers resumed their routines, but Daniel remained distracted. Shortly after boarding at Sioux City, he had noticed a young woman traveling with her mother and younger sister. Though he didn't know it during those first weeks, he later found out that her name was Nellie Sage. Nellie was a bit too sturdy to fit the prevailing Victorian ideal, but even from afar she had a manner and a glow that drew him in. Weeks had passed since they'd left Iowa, yet they hadn't met or exchanged any words. Daniel's ticket bought him little more than a space to sleep on the deck, while Nellie was a cabin passenger, which meant a private cabin and meals in a dining room with white linen and waiters. The two groups didn't easily mix, especially when a group of unaccompanied women was involved.

So, when Daniel looked up to see who had fired the shots, he was astonished to see Nellie looking in his direction, showing no interest in the unfolding events. She simply smiled and held her gaze long enough to convey that it wasn't accidental.

Nellie had also taken note of Daniel early on the voyage. She'd found him handsome enough, but that wasn't what had drawn her to him. It was the laughter. On the lower deck that had become Daniel's world, he could usually be found amid a little knot of men he had only come to know since Sioux City. Often, when Nellie allowed herself to look down, Daniel had captured the group's interest. The laughter was never far behind.

Their silent encounter was broken when Nellie's mother approached and looked down toward Daniel. She took little note of him but made clear her intention of taking Nellie to the other side of the deck.

Daniel reluctantly returned his attention to the river. To no one in particular he recited a few lines from Robert Burns, a poet his father had regularly recited, especially when the whiskey was flowing:

'Twas na her bonnie blue e'e was my ruin;
Fair tho' she be, that ne'er my undoin';
'Twas the dear smile when naebody did mind us,
'Twas the bewitching, sweet, stown glance o' kindness.

Daniel had begun his journey in New Brunswick, a stingy place where the little wealth that could be scraped from the land had been taken decades ago when the last of the big trees had been felled. Daniel left Canada in 1879, briefly stopping in western Minnesota, where the black prairie soils produced fat yields and new towns were prospering. Like so many before him, Daniel headed west not just to seek what was new, but also to leave a part of his life behind. When asked, he'd say it was a letter from a cousin that had put him on this path. But it went deeper than that. New Brunswick had become too painful a place. The previous year he had lost his wife, a sweet woman named Katie, who died in childbirth. He lost them both. Despite the passage of more than a year, the pain seemed inescapable, often arising in unpredictable ways, triggered by random events woven into daily life. After a day of intense grief, this time brought on by the fragrance of newly cut hay and memories of working their small fields together, Daniel knew he had to leave.

The letter from Daniel's cousin was filled with references to cheap land and good wages, and they were all true. Though the money was good in Montevideo, a town platted on the Minnesota prairie just a few years before Daniel's arrival, he soon realized that these flatlands offered just another version of an ordinary life filled with hard work—something he had vowed to leave behind. More than that, though, were the stories. Further west, in the mountains and prairies of Montana, the frontier persisted and fortunes were being built on the minerals and other resources that awaited discovery. Those who had been there said the opportunity to be a part of it wouldn't last much longer.

On this voyage, the *Red Cloud*'s decks were crowded with a mix of passengers, each with dreams formed by a time perhaps unlike any other, a time when an emerging modernism was juxtaposed against a backdrop of raw frontier. The telephone and other new wonders of technology were becoming commonplace, yet vast areas remained unsettled and the old ways persisted. Aboard the *Red Cloud* were more than a hundred Canadian Mounted Police recruits on their way to the still mostly lawless plains, where the northern tribes and a few reservation holdouts lived off the last of the buffalo herds. The rush to break these lands with the plow was decades away, but among the steamboat's passengers were a few cattlemen, each willing to bet on the proposition that the grass of Montana would fatten more beef than would be lost to rustlers and wolves. Others, including Daniel McHarg, were just keeping up a slow westward drift, not knowing what might turn up but hopeful that it would be better than what they had left behind.

II.

Not long after the *Red Cloud* had entered Montana Territory, the landscape seemed to announce that they were entering a different sort of place. The grassy, rounded bluffs along the lower river had gradually shed their mantle of soil, ultimately emerging as a series of stark white spires and castle-like outcrops. Though they weren't visible from the river yet, Daniel sensed that the Rockies couldn't be much further ahead, the sight of which would mark their arrival in the West. More importantly, Daniel felt, the mountains would signal an imminent end to a long and often tedious voyage. Inspired by this possibility, Daniel looked forward to the boat's next stop for wood and an opportunity to scramble up a bluff and view the horizon.

A heavily laden steamboat forcing its way upriver consumed an immense amount of wood, requiring regular stops to load a resource that had become increasingly scarce with the increase in river traffic. As she approached a little island where the valley widened, the *Red Cloud* stopped to take on wood. It was an opportunity for the passengers to get off and walk on solid ground. Daniel joined the small procession, which consisted mostly of deck passengers who were expected to assist in loading the wood on board. Daniel went to it, returning with armloads of cottonwood and pine scraped from the surrounding breaks.

A group of wood cutters, who were known as woodhawks along the Missouri, slouched in the shade and watched, enjoying a chance to see others work and perhaps to catch a glimpse of a woman. They were rough-looking men, hardened by years of difficult and dangerous work. Yet they weren't unlike other men Daniel had known in the woods of New Brunswick, a place where the 30 cords a day needed to keep a river boat running could be readily found. Here, Daniel thought, the work required to gather that much wood for the several boats plying the Upper Missouri was unimaginable.

Daniel paused between loads to talk with the woodhawks. "I hope you fellows are paid well. A lumberman could find himself a hell of a better place to work than this." The woodhawks ignored him at first, conveying the mild contempt they held for anyone who had just entered the territory. Eager to talk with someone new, Daniel persisted. "Maybe, then, you've forgotten the mother tongue way out here. Or is it that your throats are too dry to get the words out?"

Daniel offered up a small flask of whiskey, which the men quickly drained. The oldest of them, a man who was missing two fingers, responded while the others continued to gaze toward the boat. "A pilgrim like you wouldn't know it, but one of them scrawny yellow pines is as valuable here as oak wood in Boston, or whatever Yankee place you come from."

"Ah, you're confused about that, my friend," chided Daniel. "I'm not an American Yankee. That's Canada you hear, maybe with a bit of my family's beginnings in Scotland mixed in."

One of the men recalled his own Scottish ancestry and softened a little. "There used to be more trees down here by the river," he said. "Now we spend more time haulin' 'em down here than we do cutting trees. If it weren't decent money, we'd be damned fools. Look at me. How old do you think I am?"

Before Daniel could respond, the woodhawk declared that he was only twenty-two.

The others roared at this obvious falsehood, and one of them added, "Caleb was twenty-two before the war for southern independence. It's not just the hard work. Fear of the Blackfoot will age a man. Many of us have died along this river, and many have taken their last breath with the burn of a Blackfoot arrow lodged in his guts."

Another woodhawk joked that they were getting kind of lonely now that the Blackfoot usually stayed north of the Missouri. In the early 1880's, the vast Blackfoot lands stretched most of the way from the Missouri north to Canada. A few more years of pressure and clamoring by the politicians of Montana Territory would shrink it to a mere fragment before the decade was over.

Daniel bantered with the group for a few more minutes and asked if the Rockies could be seen from higher up the ridge. One of the woodhawks responded, "There's a little range called the Bear Paws nearby. You can see them on a clear day. But unless you want to walk from here to Fort Benton, you'd better get your ass back on the boat." Daniel shrugged and urged the woodhawks to watch their backs before walking back to the Red Cloud, whose crew was already making ready to push off.

The *Red Cloud* continued upriver for the remainder of the day, until it finally reached a suitable bank to tie up for the night. Daniel and the rest of the passengers hoped this would be their last night on the river. On most nights, if the weather was clear, Daniel preferred to sleep on land. He held no affection for the crowded boat and was glad he'd soon be done with her. He was rolling out his bedding and intently kicking away a few prickly pears when he looked up to see a young woman walking toward him. She smiled awkwardly, trying to cover her embarrassment about approaching a man like this.

"I didn't want to leave this boat without knowing your name," she said. "I'm Nellie Sage."

"And I'm Daniel McHarg." A brief silence ensued. Neither knew what to say next—even Daniel, who always seemed to have the right words at hand.

"What will you do in Fort Benton?" Nellie asked after an awkward pause. Before Daniel could answer, she added, "My father sent for us from Helena. He owns one of the mines in the area. We'll be in Fort Benton only a short while. Once we get settled in Helena, I'll probably help my sister with the school."

"Well, that's more of a plan than I have." Daniel thought further. "They say this land isn't all used up yet. I'm planning to look for some gold. Or maybe something else, something I haven't even thought of yet." He smiled broadly before adding, "If nothing else turns up, I can always get by banging on some nails. But I didn't come all this way for that."

Nellie glanced back at the boat. Her mother and sister would be looking for her soon. "Well, I've done what I can do. I hope you prosper in this new land of yours, Mr. McHarg." She turned and began walking briskly to the boat.

Daniel savored the sight of her movement before adding, "I hope to prosper, Miss Nellie Sage, but I'll settle for a chance to see you again."

Nellie paused to look back at Daniel, and that look changed Daniel's world.

III.

On the next day the *Red Cloud* reached Coal Banks
Landing. A great herd of horses had been assembled
onshore to take the Canadian Mounted Police north to
Fort Macleod. Daniel watched with amusement as his
countrymen, who had enjoyed a temporary relaxing of
military discipline on the trip upriver, resumed a stiff
formality. They were greeted by a Captain Kincaide,
who reminded them that they were in the service of the
Queen and that their job was to keep American whiskey
out of Canada and the Cree and other tribes north of
the border. For centuries the border had meant little to
the tribes that inhabited the northern plains, but in time
they had learned that U.S. troops would not pursue
their raiding parties past an imaginary line, which they
began calling the Medicine Line. To the cattlemen of
Montana Territory, the raiding parties from the north
were "British Indians," and the cattlemen's outrage over
livestock losses built throughout much of the 1880s.

It took longer than planned to unload the troops and
their gear. By the time the boat moved on, the light was
beginning to fade. The *Red Cloud* made only a few
more miles before the captain decided to tie up again
for the night.

On the final day, Daniel and the other passengers who
were on their first trip to Montana Territory spent the
morning looking expectantly upriver. Daniel predicted
that each new bend would be the last, but it would only
reveal another wild landscape lacking any suggestion
of a town.

Just below Fort Benton, the river makes a big bend, following a course through a series of narrow channels studded with islands and sandbars. In most places, the Upper Missouri is a river that seems mild mannered. But it's a hard river to read and often deceptively treacherous. In most places, the river was wide and deep enough for a steamboat's easy passage. But sometimes, unseen until nearly upon it, the channel would split and force a hard choice. One channel brought safe passage, while the other could rip open a hull with a cottonwood snag lurking just below the waterline. The good river men had an instinct for these hazards but even the best of them were not infallible. The scores of wrecks embedded in the Missouri's shifting channel provided stark evidence of the risks.[1]

The *Red Cloud* was one of the larger boats that worked the Upper Missouri and she was tantalizingly close to Fort Benton when she hit a sandbar. Her powerful engine couldn't budge her from the river's grip. It wasn't the first time this had happened, so there wasn't a general panic. Instead, the passengers clustered where they could get a good view of the crew's vigorous efforts to free the boat, wary of evoking their wrath by getting in the way. Like all the boats plying the Upper Missouri, the *Red Cloud* was equipped with an odd-looking apparatus that allowed her to "walk" over a bar using an elaborate series of wooden spars and pulleys to lift the boat off the river bottom. It was an ingenious system when it worked well, but on this day the crew's initial efforts only succeeded in rocking the *Red Cloud*'s massive hull a slight distance and embedding her further into the mire.

---

[1] The *Red Cloud*'s trip upriver in 1882 proved to be its last successful voyage. On the way back to St. Louis, she struck a snag about 200 miles below Fort Benton and quickly sank.

Amid the commotion, Daniel found himself standing close to Nellie. Gladdened by an unexpected chance to see each other again but burdened by the knowledge that their time was short, they shared a few observations about the activity to free the boat. As they parted, Nellie told Daniel that she and her sister would be in Fort Benton for a few days before leaving for Helena. Daniel immediately began to think about how he'd manage to see her again.

Just as it seemed the Red Cloud might break free, one of the spars snapped into pieces, sending a few large splinters into the air. The boat settled back into the bar. It took nearly an hour to mount a new spar, which this time provided enough lift for the boat to reverse the paddle wheel, a procedure that effectively dammed the water near the hull and sometimes allowed a boat to float free. It worked, and the Red Cloud moved back into the channel amid a chorus of cheers.

Finally, after a bit more traveling, the Red Cloud pushed through a bend that brought Fort Benton into view. The captain let loose a series of whistle blasts and a rousing cheer came up from the decks. The Red Cloud pushed past two other boats that were tied up along the levee and stopped near the town's impressive new hotel still under construction.

The town edged up to the Missouri's north bank and marked the head of navigation on this remarkable river. Its location so far inland and utter isolation prompted more than one traveler to think it an apparition. In the early days, like much of the western frontier, Fort Benton was a place where community builders and outlaws, preachers and ruffians, lived side by side. It wasn't always clear which side would win out. Even so, the town had long been a vital place. Before the arrival of the railroads, steamboats transported nearly everything that entered or exited the interior Northwest—and none of the boats could make it further upriver than Fort Benton.

Even with the heavy river traffic of the past decade, the arrival of a steamer was a major event. Long-awaited shipments, friends not seen for months or even years, new people to gawk at, and news from the outside world combined to stir up the town. Many of Fort Benton's inhabitants stood along Front Street as the *Red Cloud* pulled up to the levee and set out its lines.

Daniel was traveling lighter than most passengers and was among the first to leave the boat. He was confident that he'd have time to seek out Nellie the following day, after she settled into her hotel. As he shouldered his bag, John Campbell, another Canadian from the Maritimes, hailed him. John was a fellow deck passenger and one of the men Daniel had come to know best during the journey.

"It's the saloon I'm headed for, Daniel," said John. "We deserve a snoot-full tonight, I'm thinking."

Daniel had been practically bred to the taste of whiskey, but at the moment he had other things on his mind and felt a need to get away from the crowd. "I'll find you in a while, Johnny," he called to his friend. "Try to pick out a place where we won't get shot."

Daniel set off along Front Street, determined to get a feel for this Montana, a place he hoped would be his last stop. Along with the curious and those waiting to greet family and friends, the levee was crowded with porters and hustlers for all manner of services. Daniel pushed past them all and seized the first opportunity to climb out of the confined river valley and see the country beyond. As he walked briskly through town, he noted all the construction underway and felt some relief from the knowledge that he could always find work here if nothing else panned out.

North of Fort Benton, the land slopes gently up to a ridge more than two hundred feet above the river. Daniel pointed himself in that direction and followed a swale that meandered through the treeless grasslands. From the heights, he looked out on a vast landscape, one dominated by short grass in every direction. The land was irregular, rising and falling with no apparent pattern, except where the river had cut down through it and exposed a series of stark, barren cliffs. Isolated ranges rose from the plains here and there, the closest of which were the Highwoods to the south. Daniel lingered on a high spot and tried to see some glimmer of destiny, a hint of a new life beyond the distant hills. It wasn't to be seen that day. Instead, as he looked out over a vast and completely unfamiliar landscape, he felt the pain return. Before the pain could sink in too far, he forced himself to remember that this was a special day and it was time to join the boys and celebrate their arrival in Fort Benton.

Daniel found John Campbell in the Antlers, one of the numerous saloons that lined the levee along the riverfront. Many of them were rough looking places but a few were graced with a touch of civility, such as an upright piano or a portrait of Lincoln. The Antlers had both of these touches, along with an ornate bar brought upriver from St. Louis. John was with a small group of men, most of whom wore an expression of wonderment that made them look out of place. The expressions were genuine, for the group largely consisted of newcomers just arrived on the *Red Cloud*. Among them, however, was a man Daniel had not seen before, an older man who dominated the conversation. He wore a bright red shirt and a gold pendant, items chosen to announce that he was no ordinary man. The stranger winced from time to time, especially when he rose from his chair. His wincing, Daniel would soon learn, resulted from the pain of a terrible old wound.

Daniel greeted John and the others warmly, who pronounced that Daniel would have to drink fast if he wanted to catch up. The older stranger ignored Daniel at first and resumed the tale that Daniel's arrival had interrupted. It was a story of gold prospecting and narrow escapes. Occasionally, the man paused the story at a suspenseful moment, which the newcomers had learned would require the purchase of another whiskey for the story to resume.

Daniel listened patiently for a while, but this wasn't the celebration he expected at the end of a long voyage. By the next break in the story, Daniel had reached his limit. "I don't know about the rest of you, but I'm tired of such seriousness," he said, and began to lay out a drinking wager. The prospector, loathe to give up the group's full attention, began to interrupt, but Daniel waved him off. "Let's have a little wager," Daniel continued. "I'll buy any man a drink if he can do a simple exercise. Any man who tries it but fails buys me one. Do I have any takers?"

There were murmurs of agreement. The prospector, however, uttered a few cusses in Daniel's direction.

"Now hold on there, pal," John Campbell interjected. "You've got no cause to insult my friend Daniel." John was a big man who had become protective of Daniel after a scrape they had gotten into during an unplanned stop in Bismarck.

Daniel could see that despite John's efforts, there would be no celebration as long as the prospector's dominance persisted. He tried to deter the stranger with an offer. "Here's a proposition, my friend—"

"Call me Limestone," the prospector cut in.

"Very well, Limestone. You'll get an equal share of my winnings, which I assure you will be considerable. All you have to do is enjoy the free whiskey."

Sensing that he had nothing to lose, the prospector finally nodded.

Daniel moved to the center of the room and made a small show of taking off his jacket. "We can all bend our knees, squat, and get up again," he began. "It's a familiar act. But try it on one leg." With that, Daniel extended his left leg horizontally and lowered himself to the floor. After holding that position for a few seconds, he smoothly rose back to full height. "Now, who wants a free drink for doing such a simple thing?"

There were plenty of takers. Men of all sizes, each confident in his ability to match Daniel's maneuver, made the effort, and all of them failed. Some made it halfway up before falling back on their haunches. Others crumpled to the floor before they could make it to a crouching position. Every attempt provoked much anticipation from the man up next and many of them boasted about how easy they would make it look. Neither Daniel nor the hard-drinking prospector could keep up with the free drinks that kept coming his way. After a few rounds, both men put their winnings back on the table for any takers.

After the action slowed and the liquor settled in, Limestone sensed another opportunity to hold the group's attention. He pulled a piece of dark metal from his pocket and dropped it onto the table without comment, confident that questions would soon follow. In response to the first, Limestone said only one word: "Shiloh." Then, after a pause, he went on. "It was a brutal fight. Both sides threw everything they had at each other. The doctors pulled this chunk of metal out of my hip but another piece was buried deep. They said they could get it out, but it might kill me on the spot. I decided to take my chances and leave it in." Limestone paused, then added, "If this thing kills me tomorrow, I figure I won that bet!"

More questions followed and Limestone was happy to resume his tale. "On the last day of the fight, the man next to me was split open, and I went down too. At first I thought I was the lucky one, but I had no feeling in my legs and couldn't crawl without an unbearable pain somewhere in my gut. No one came for us. I lay there all night and listened to the others beg for help. By morning there were no other sounds. With a swollen tongue and the belief that my own death was just a matter of time, I began to envy my friend's quick death."

The group listened intently to Limestone's tale. When Daniel thought it might have run its course, he brought up gold prospecting again, a topic Limestone was happy to return to. By the end of the night, the group had bonded deeply—but the biggest winner was the house, which realized twice the sales of a normal Tuesday night. Finally, after a few men had slumped into their chairs, the group broke up. Glad that there were only a few streets to choose from, Daniel drifted back up the hill, slipped into the boardinghouse where he had dropped his gear, and collapsed into the oblivion that always followed the whiskey.

IV.

Daniel awoke from a vigorous shaking, grimaced at the bright light of midday, and looked up to see Limestone, who urged him to gather his gear and head out to the mountains. Daniel was about to lash out when Limestone reminded him of the arrangements they had made the previous night.

Daniel responded, "I recall agreeing to go with you, old man, but I didn't say anything about when."

"Daniel, the time is right. I've got a good feeling about this, something I haven't had for a while. So let's get started, and we'll find that lode I told you about."

Daniel forced himself into a greater awareness and was struck by the realization that he hadn't located Nellie and wasn't sure when she was leaving for Helena. Ignoring Limestone's plea, Daniel asked, "Where's a rich man's daughter likely to stay in this town?"

Limestone was tempted to have some fun with Daniel, but hesitated when he saw how serious his new friend had become. "Just head down Front Street, and you'll see it. Most of the other places . . . well, let's just say that a rich man wouldn't put his family in any of them."

Now more aware of the pounding in his head, Daniel splashed some water on his face, told Limestone he'd be back later, and left abruptly. He headed straight for the riverfront and entered the lobby of the hotel Limestone had described. A uniformed bellman eyed Daniel as he pushed past the doors. Upon reaching the front desk, Daniel confidently asked the desk clerk if the Sage family was in residence.

"They were here last night," the clerk responded, "but they all took the morning stage to Helena." The clerk saw a look of great disappointment descend on Daniel's face. "I'm sorry, but that was more than three hours ago."

Daniel turned to leave. As he neared the front door he heard the deskman call his name.

"Might you be Mr. Daniel McHarg? I have a note for someone by that name."

Daniel nodded and took the note from the deskman. Though he feared the worst, the sight of Nellie's fine hand writing on the envelope brought a sliver of hope, just enough to allow himself to imagine the possibility that Nellie's departure was not an abrupt ending to something that had become very important. Despite his eagerness to read the note, he first walked across Front Street to the river and sat on one of the many crates that lined the levee, most of which were awaiting shipment to the mines.

The note was addressed to Mr. Daniel McHarg in a flowing script. He opened the envelope carefully and read its contents:

Dear Mr. McHarg: I regret that we had to leave Fort Benton sooner than anticipated. We had intended to visit with my aunt who resides here, but my father was unexpectedly in town to greet us. He had urgent business back in Helena and insisted that we all leave with him the day following our arrival.

I don't know how this may occur, but my hope is that Montana is not so large as to prevent our meeting again.

> *Yours very truly,*
> *Nellie Sage*

Daniel walked back to the boardinghouse. He was so preoccupied with thoughts of Nellie that he was almost surprised to see Limestone sitting on the porch, obscured by a cloud of smoke rising from an oddly shaped pipe. He looked older in the morning light—his face was marked by creases and a few scars but his eyes shone with an eagerness for life.

"Well, Daniel," said Limestone, "looks like you've come to your senses and decided to make yourself rich."

Daniel was far from ready to let go of Nellie, but he knew that chasing her to Helena might not do any good. No, he'd have to figure out the right approach, which would be easier to do if this expedition of Limestone's paid off. Daniel knew full well that Nellie lived in a world different from his and that anything he could do to narrow the gap separating them might enhance his prospects. He returned his attention to the prospector. "All right, Limestone, where's this gold you've been talking about? Where are we going?"

"The Judith Mountains," Limestone replied. "I've got a good hunch about a particular place I saw last year. I don't know if it's got a name, but I call it Jackass Gulch on account of the carcass I saw there last time."

Though Jackass Gulch didn't sound like an auspicious name, Daniel let it go. Instead, he pursued his curiosity about the Judith Mountains, an unfamiliar range that also, he thought, bore a peculiar name. "Who was this Judith, Limestone?" he asked. "Why'd someone name those mountains after her?"

Limestone was happy to point out that as with many places in Montana, the name of the Judith Mountains originated with the Lewis and Clark expedition. "Judith was Clark's sweetheart, and a special one she must have been," he informed Daniel. "Anyway, we'll start near Jackass Gulch, but I've seen traces of gold throughout that country. Besides, Daniel, a man could do a lot worse with his time than wander through the Judith Mountains in summer. It's beautiful country."

Daniel was thinking of a different kind of beauty, but he nodded before adding, "One more thing. I just got here. Whatever gold is lying in those mountains will still be there in a few days. I've been sitting on a damn boat for the past month, and I've hardly seen this town."

In protest, Limestone pointed out that what had brought Daniel to Montana was out in the mountains, not in a crowded town. But in the end they agreed to take the stage to Maiden at the beginning of the following week.

For the next few days Daniel watched the comings and goings on the waterfront and listened to the talk in the bars. In addition to the usual rumors of where gold was being found, there was talk of another type of boom: the imminent cattle boom. Though the local market for beef remained small, the railroad was coming, and its arrival would change everything. The vast grasslands of Montana were there for the taking, the talk went, and would bring riches to those who took a chance on the land.

Inspired partly by the local commentary, but perhaps more by an immediate desire to wander outside the town, Daniel and John Campbell rode north one afternoon. They soon came upon the wide valley of the Teton River, which rose far to the west among the great peaks of the Continental Divide. Near Fort Benton the Teton is a plains river, richly lined with cottonwoods and hemmed in by low bluffs. Amid the cottonwoods the valley seemed almost lush, offering deep soils and shelter from the harsh Montana winds. Daniel was moved by the setting, which inspired in him a feeling he'd felt before. Some places could take hold of a man, he knew, and even make him see the world differently.

After wandering across the river and downstream a few miles, Daniel and John rode back on top, pausing to look back at the valley from time to time.

V.

Three Blackfoot men were riding south and had almost reached the Missouri River when they saw a group of vultures circling overhead, effortlessly gliding in the afternoon updrafts, gathering their numbers in a series of tightening concentric circles. The object of their interest was a dead buffalo that had washed up on the shore and become stranded by the quickly lowering river flows that followed the June rise. Despite the stench, the men closely inspected the carcass and noted that the animal had been shot and not simply drowned. Two of the men wondered how such a thing could happen, but the oldest of the group, Follows Bear, said he had heard that the white men sometimes shot animals from their "fire boats" and let the bodies drift away with the current.

One of Follows Bear's companions, a fierce-looking man known as Looks Beyond, became quiet, his anger deepening as he contemplated how everything was changing and how much had been lost. He broke the silence forcefully: "They do not belong here. The white men do not belong here!"

Earlier that year, the buffalo hunt had been successful. Expecting the same result on the next hunt, the three Blackfoot men had set off to scout the locations of the herds. They had traveled many days without sighting any buffalo, all the way to the standing rocks that marked the descent to the Big River. They had become more anxious with each passing day.

Until the very end, few Blackfoot—especially those who shunned the government handouts and clung to traditional ways—could imagine the possibility that the 1881–1882 hunt would be the last successful hunt. It was inconceivable that something so ingrained in life itself and abundant beyond counting, could vanish forever. It was no more likely than the grass ceasing to grow or the stars ceasing to glow in the sky.

VI.

As planned, Daniel met Limestone at the upper ferry, where the river flowed past a dark cliff nearly black where it met the floodplain. The gloomy setting added a sense of foreboding to the venture they were about to undertake. The ferry was a simple affair, just large enough to hold the stage and its team. A system of cables pulled them across the river.

It felt odd to be on the water again. Daniel was reminded of the seemingly endless days he had spent traveling on the *Red Cloud*. Soon, though, as the stage crept up a tight little cleft in the bluffs, scarcely faster than a man could walk, he was reminded of the advantages of river travel. These advantages would become even more evident as the day wore on. Daniel and the others endured hours at a stretch in a cramped cabin, jolted by a rough road. The stiff springs of the carriage did little to soften the ride. Daniel was in a pensive mood, brought on by the knowledge that he was heading east, a direction that would take him even farther from Nellie.

In addition to Daniel and Limestone, the stage held two other passengers and the driver, who, like most everyone else in town, was acquainted with Limestone. Now and again, when the ride was quiet and the road smooth, Limestone and the driver would yell back and forth. Their conversation came in little bursts followed by periods of silence. In one exchange, the driver mocked Limestone's ability to find anything of value, much less gold: "The only gold Limestone's ever been close to was in someone else's pocket."

Limestone quickly retorted to the group. "Has anyone noticed that we're in the company of the ugliest stage driver in Montana Territory? He's so ugly that he has to put blinders on his horses to keep them from bolting when he walks by."

It went on like that most of the morning.

Just when the travelers were reaching the limit of their endurance, a prominent landmark came into view. "There she is: Grizzly Butte!" Limestone proclaimed. The butte was a welcome signal of a station ahead, a place that offered rest and a meal and a chance to get out of the little box that had confined them since Fort Benton.

The station stood just off the road and presented a rude appearance. It consisted of a few sheds, some corrals, and a low log building with a sod roof. They were greeted by a stout woman named Anna, who dressed plainly and spoke with a German accent. She had a Teutonic formality that gave her personality an edge, one honed by the need for a woman who was often alone or greatly outnumbered by men to keep them at a certain distance. Limestone and the stage driver knew of her no-nonsense reputation and remained unusually subdued.

As Anna served up a meal of cold meats, bread, and beer, she gazed at one of the passengers carrying a small case and pointed to it with a look of recognition. She pronounced it a violin and requested that he play. The man, who was on his way to Chicago to play with an orchestra that summer, initially declined, but his fellow passengers urged him on further. Anna's offer of a brand name whiskey on the house provided the final bit of persuasion needed. The man carefully removed the instrument from its case and performed a minor ritual of limbering the bow and making a few adjustments to the strings. Once ready to play, he began with a few vigorous strokes, producing an intensity of sound that startled his little audience in the confined space of the stage stop.

The music settled into a melodic sequence. Daniel and the other travelers recognized none of it but were drawn into its elegance and the clarity with which the man played. Focused intently on the violinist, the group was distracted only by a suppressed sob from Anna, who wiped a tear from her cheek in apparent embarrassment.

By the time the piece was over, Daniel and the others were also moved. They hesitated before applauding, but Anna immediately beamed her approval and complimented his playing of a difficult piece, Bach's "Air on a G String". Then, because she had a reputation to maintain—especially in front of the stage driver—Anna felt compelled to explain her sentimentality. "When I was a child in Munich, we attended a concert nearly every Sunday. I haven't heard this music for many, many years. When I listen, I'm a girl again and my family is still close." She gestured with open arms to the dimly lit space and the primitive furniture before adding, "Now I have only this."

Though Anna didn't speak of it, Limestone and the stage driver knew that she was still waiting for her husband, who had never returned from a solo hunting trip the previous year. Everyone but Anna assumed he was dead. Anna clung to a hope. On some days, she felt it was the only thing she had left.

By the time they reached Maiden, a newly risen town at the edge of the Judith Mountains, it was nearly dark and the group was weary. Still, Limestone insisted on going to a saloon, where the talk was about who had come and gone, new claims, and feuds. Daniel felt like an outsider and soon tired of it. As he headed to the hotel, Limestone called out, "Now, Daniel, remember this night and what it feels like to go to bed a poor man. You haven't many of these nights left."

The next day was clear and brilliant. Daniel awoke early and walked along the town's main street. Maiden was a beehive of activity, with heavy freight wagons moving equipment up the mountain to the mines. Though many buildings had sprung up, the town retained a raw appearance. Everything was new but roughly constructed with minimal ornamentation. The main street was rutted and muddy with an occasional plank thrown across some of the larger depressions. Still, there were stores with nearly everything you'd want to buy and more than enough saloons. Before turning back to roust Limestone, Daniel paused and looked up, past a devastated forest, to the spoil piles and scars on the mountain. "Someone like us probably stumbled onto that ore body," he thought. "Maybe it'll happen again."

For the remainder of the morning, Daniel and Limestone acquired the necessities for their expedition. They bought supplies and a few basic items, but their biggest purchase was the horses. Limestone insisted that a breeder named Brooks, who lived along Warm Springs Creek, raised horses that were better suited for the mountains than any of the stock they could get in Fort Benton. After much discussion and some bargaining, they purchased two saddle horses and a larger pack animal. Daniel's anticipation grew, but even though Limestone paid his share of the costs, Daniel's excitement was tempered by the knowledge that the money he had saved wouldn't last long at this rate.

Once the transactions were completed, Limestone headed them further north. Limestone, who knew the country well and exulted to be in the mountains again, pointed out an occasional landmark to Daniel. They traveled slowly, for Limestone took time to observe the land intently. They stopped occasionally to take a few swings of their picks against an outcrop Limestone had judged to be promising or to peer behind a boulder lodged in a stream where gold flakes tended to settle out. They made only a few miles that afternoon and camped on a knoll where they could see for miles in nearly every direction.

Over the next several days, their routine didn't vary. They arose early but lingered in camp and drank coffee as they waited for the sun to rise above the ridge and bring more warmth to the land. A trace of placer gold here and there kept them motivated, but in those first days there were no signs of the major ore body Limestone had targeted. By evening they were tired and stiff but happy to settle by the fire and feast on elk steaks cut from a cow Limestone had shot earlier in the day. Limestone enhanced the meat with a gravy of flour, grease from the pan, stream water, and a few herbs plucked from the shrubs they passed on their daily travels. Before drifting off to sleep, they'd talk on a wide range of subjects. Limestone had a repertoire of stories from the wild years he'd spent in places like Bannock and Virginia City, where, lured west by news of gold strikes and a determination to leave behind the bloody mess of the war, he had arrived in late 1862. He also spoke of more practical matters, introducing Daniel to the people, geography, and ways of this new land. Limestone delivered all his tales with the usual braggadocio and humor, yet Daniel realized he was getting a serious education not easily acquired in any other way.

Although Limestone dominated most conversations, he often prompted Daniel to talk about his life in faraway New Brunswick, which Daniel gladly obliged. Inevitably, after Daniel shared a tale about the time he had spent at sea or the challenges faced by the the Loyalists who settled New Brunswick, Limestone would take a good-natured jab at Daniel's lack of knowledge about anything a prospector needed to know: "You stick close to me, Daniel. You've got a lot to learn about this country, and you'll do well to listen closely to the bountiful wisdom that flows from your partner."

Near the end of the week, following a fine breakfast of trout fried in bacon grease and flour, they moved further north to try another ridge. Limestone's mood was buoyed by the fine weather and his delight at being back in the Judith country. "Far as I'm concerned," he remarked, "just the chance of being in a place like this makes a man rich. I've found a bit of gold in my time. But even if I never found anything, I'd still be doing this."

After they set out that day, Limestone maintained his usual chatter. He pointed out unconformities and other geologic features that might give some clues about the minerals below. Daniel, who was less experienced at riding on steep terrain, held the reins tight and moved cautiously as his horse picked its way across the stony ground.

Soon after they started down an unremarkable slope, Limestone's horse slipped and put him on the ground. At first it seemed like a minor mishap. The horse stood up quickly, and Limestone did the same. He brushed himself off and quipped about the sure-footed horses he had insisted on buying. Within moments, though, the color began to leave Limestone's face, and, declaring that he hadn't broken any bones but was feeling a little squishy inside, he sat back down. Both men began to suspect that the jarring had moved the shrapnel buried in his body.

Their suspicions were confirmed when Limestone spat up some blood. By late morning he became very weak. Daniel moved him carefully into the shade of a pine and comforted him for the remainder of the day. Occasionally Daniel suggested that he head back to Maiden for help, but Limestone would have none of it. He maintained a calm that came from a belief that he was destined to die in this manner.

Even in his weakened condition, Limestone was talkative. Again he told Daniel of the days when the range held only buffalo and no roads scarred the prairie. Now the cattle were here, and soon there would be more towns and even farmers. "I'm not sure I want to live long enough to see it," Limestone pronounced before drifting off into a fitful sleep.

By nightfall they both knew he was dying. Though the evening was warm, Limestone began to shiver. Even after Daniel built a fire and wrapped him in his bedding, the prospector's shivering continued.

"I may not make it through this night, Daniel," said Limestone, "and there's something I want to give you before I'm gone." With discomfort, he reached into the small pouch he always carried and handed Daniel the metal fragment pulled from his body twenty years earlier at Shiloh.

Daniel hesitated and then joked, "If I'd known you were going to give me this, I'd have tripped you myself."

Even in his grave condition, Limestone saw the humor in Daniel's remark. "You're catching on, Daniel, but listen now. This is important." Limestone went on to describe how to get to the home of an old and trusted friend, a man who lived along the Judith River just a few miles above the Missouri. "Give him this, Daniel. Jean Baptiste will know it's from me. If he's still alive, he'll give you a package, something I've had him hold for me."

Daniel felt a burden being placed upon him. He doubted that a man who worked so hard to get others to pick up his bar bills could have anything of value hidden away. "Why not let Jean Baptiste keep it?" Daniel asked.

"LaValle? Well, I've never known a man who cared so little for possessions. You take it. I want you to have something from me."

Daniel promised he'd go to visit LaValle, mostly because Limestone wanted him to. Any expectation of personal gain was secondary.

By morning, Limestone was gone. Daniel took his body into Maiden. While he was there, someone sent for the sheriff, who took Daniel's statement. The sheriff knew Limestone well and had no reason to doubt Daniel's account. He asked to see the body and quickly concluded that there were no obvious wounds or other evidence of foul play. But the sight of Limestone's body, laid out on a table and eerily white, shook Daniel from the determination he had mustered to focus on getting his companion to Maiden. Now the finality of Limestone's death fully sank in, and Daniel realized that he had lost a great friend and mentor.

A reporter from Fort Benton's *River Press, who* regularly sent a dispatch from the region's biggest boomtown, had heard the buzz around Maiden. He made sure to get an interview with both Daniel and the sheriff. The whole experience left Daniel shaken. He was no longer eager to prospect, at least not in the mountains where Limestone had just died.

VII.

Helena had settled in to her glory days. The once-rambunctious mining camp was becoming respectable and comfortably wealthy. Rather than focusing only on mineral wealth, the townspeople had turned their energy to the business of mining, and the mine owners and bankers had built dozens of impressive homes at the foot of Mount Helena. Among them, on Dearborn Avenue was the Sage residence, a two-story Victorian with a sweeping porch and graceful lines. Following a late breakfast, Nellie and her sister Helen, a schoolteacher, sat in a sunny room to consider their day. Nellie stared idly out the window while Helen read the local newspaper. They sat together quietly, the silence broken by Helen's occasional comment on an article she thought might also interest Nellie.

"Hey, Nellie, here's something. A poor man died, and the article mentions a Mr. Daniel McHarg, who came up on the *Red Cloud*. I don't believe we met him, but—"

Nellie cut her off in alarm. "Oh, my god, Helen, is he dead?"

Puzzled by Nellie's reaction, Helen responded, "No, it's not Mr. McHarg who died. Let me read it to you."

"We were saddened to learn this week of the unfortunate death of Limestone Smith. Mr. Smith, who was known throughout much of Montana Territory, died while prospecting in the mountains north of Maiden. The immediate cause of death was a fall from his horse. In a real sense, though, he was a casualty of the civil war. The wound he suffered at Shiloh finally killed him. He served the cause of the Union admirably and will be remembered fondly by all who knew him. Limestone's body was brought into town by his partner, Mr. Daniel McHarg, a new comer to this country who came up river this season on the Red Cloud. Mr. McHarg plans to return to Fort Benton." [First printed in the *River Press*, July 23, 1882.]

Eager to learn more about her sister's reaction, Helen continued, "Who is this Mr. McHarg, Nellie, and why are you so interested in him?"

Nellie tried to explain, though she herself was unsure how to answer Helen's second question. All in all, she concluded, it didn't really matter why. It was more important just to acknowledge that she was interested and that she had thought of Daniel often since leaving Fort Benton.

By the end of their conversation that morning, Nellie had convinced Helen to accompany her to Fort Benton. "Even if nothing comes of it," Nellie said, "I need some time away from this house. I can't stand another day of Father needing to know about everything I do. Come with me, Helen. You don't start school for another month, and we can stay with Aunt Betsy. If you agree to come, I know Father will let us go."

VIII.

It took a few days to make all the arrangements for Limestone and to put him in the ground with dignity. Daniel left Maiden the day after the burial. He was still focused on following Limestone's final wish: to seek out Limestone's friend Jean Baptiste LaValle, a reclusive man who lived far from anywhere along the lower Judith River. As Daniel descended from the mountains, the views opened up to the spreading plains, their vastness streaked by the long shadows painted by the low morning sun. For the rest of the morning he kept to the northwest as he rode across the broken grasslands. The light air had a luminous clarity that compressed distances, making it possible to see individual trees on mountain slopes miles away. From a low ridge Daniel spotted a wispy plume of dust that marked the movement of a herd of cattle, one of the arrivals from Texas, still thin from the journey across a thousand miles of the more arid lands to the south.

He made it to the lower reaches of the Judith River in the fading light of a long summer day and continued downstream toward the Missouri, hoping he hadn't missed LaValle's place and that he'd reach it before full dark. Finally, a cabin appeared among a grove of cottonwoods, a smoky cooking fire betraying its presence from the distance.

Daniel approached cautiously and hailed at regular intervals, no doubt long before his voice could be heard. First he heard the dogs, and then a voice emerged from the near darkness. The voice sounded strangely familiar. In a sense it was familiar, for Jean Baptiste retained a French accent that reflected his youth in Quebec. It was an accent often heard in the Canada Daniel had left behind.

Jean Baptiste had come upriver the hard way, pulling a flat boat laden with supplies for the American Fur Company. The work was brutal, and the years working the towropes had left his thick shoulders scarred. For the first few years he had tried to be a company man, but he soon felt too confined by even their limited direction on where to go and what to do. He adopted the life of a free trader, roaming the northern mountains and keeping to himself much of the time. But living in the land of the Blackfoot required their tolerance and a certain amount of interaction with them, which he achieved by marrying a young Blackfoot woman. Through it all, he developed a fearlessness and a fierce independence shared by few other men.

For such a man, Daniel's arrival near dark caused no immediate concern. Jean Baptiste calmly greeted Daniel with a request that he come up and join him for supper. LaValle was now well over sixty years of age, with a slight stoop that exaggerated his already short stature. Still, his broad chest and thick shoulders marked him as a man of great physical strength. Like many who took to the mountains, he had little need for company but enjoyed it when an occasional opportunity arose.

Daniel walked up to the cabin and introduced himself as a friend of Limestone. Jean Baptiste beamed at the mention of the name and immediately inquired as to Limestone's whereabouts.

Daniel felt an unexpected dread in bringing the bad news. "I buried him near Maiden yesterday morning," he said softly.

Jean Baptiste winced and turned away toward the cabin. He paused for a moment before urging Daniel to join him on one of the hewed logs that served as an outdoor bench. After they sat, Jean Baptiste stated simply, "Tell me more."

Daniel told the whole story, going back to his first encounter with Limestone at the Antlers. Jean Baptiste listened intently. When Daniel finished, Jean Baptiste nodded and finally broke his silence. "Limestone always expected he'd go like this. 'I'm living on borrowed time,' he'd say, and he lived like that too. There's only one thing to do now."

Jean Baptiste headed into the cabin and returned with a ceramic jug of whiskey. The lack of glasses prevented them from toasting their friend formally, but Jean Baptiste seemed to know of no other way to drink. They drank to a man who had cheated death for many years and had led a life worth living. When Jean

Baptiste ran out of tributes, he told Daniel more about his life as a free trader and his marriage to a beautiful Blackfoot woman. A few hours of this was all Daniel could manage. Eventually he drifted to sleep, leaving Jean Baptiste alone with the jug and his memories.

Daniel awoke to the sounds of cooking and the smell of hot grease. Jean Baptiste was occupied with cooking but had kept an eye turned to Daniel in an attempt to time the meal with his awakening. Decades of a rough life far from settlement hadn't lessened the importance he placed on eating well, a habit he considered a French birthright.

Jean Baptiste immediately noted the movement and greeted Daniel almost cheerily, promising that the buffalo liver he was frying was just the thing for a hangover.

Slowly at first, but with increasing vigor, Daniel ate a breakfast of select buffalo cuts, including the liver, and fried bread with a bone-marrow spread. For a time they limited their conversation to food. Jean Baptiste was grateful for each compliment Daniel sent his way. Near the end of the meal, Jean Baptiste praised the shaggy beast. "I have eaten the meat of every animal with a fur and some without. There is no better meat than that of the buffalo." Daniel noted that he had seen none on his trip from Maiden and only a few on the voyage up the river. "You are right Daniel, and what a pity", Jean Baptiste replied. "But they are still thick to the north, where even an old man like myself can hunt them. And sometimes, my Blackfoot friends bring me some from the Milk River country." Neither man knew that even these remaining herds would soon face the same intense assault that had annihilated the once vast herds to the south.

As LaValle cleared the table, Daniel fished in his pocket for the metal shard from Shiloh and placed it on the table. Jean Baptiste immediately recognized it. "So, Limestone told you of the package I've kept for him," he said. "Did he tell you what it is?"

Daniel assumed Jean Baptiste knew what the package was. He began to wonder if Jean Baptiste would play a game with him and deny that it contained something of value. Jean Baptiste noticed Daniel's discomfort, rose quickly, and went inside the cabin. He returned with a tightly sealed wooden box and placed it on the table. Daniel suggested they open it, but Jean Baptiste refused. "No, open it later, after you leave," he said.

After that Jean Baptiste became less talkative. Daniel feared that he had offended the old trapper, but that wasn't it. Jean Baptiste had simply reached his tolerance for sharing the confined spaces of his cabin.

Daniel left soon after breakfast. He worked his way out of the valley and ascended to yet another bench, which promised an easy passage across a long expanse of nearly flat grassland. With little need to guide his horse, he began to think about the contents of the box, but the setting was too exposed to pause and open it. He waited until he had more cover, which he found in a coulee hidden from sight and shaded by a juniper. Then he loosened the box's ties and slid off the lid.

The box held an assortment of gold nuggets, some bigger than a child's marbles, and several small bottles filled with gold flakes. It was the accumulation of most of Limestone's years of prospecting throughout Montana. Daniel was so amazed by his good fortune that his feet began to move in a little jig while his arms swept upward, his joy punctuated by an almost involuntary shout of appreciation to Limestone. After this little celebration, Daniel carefully tucked the box back into his saddlebag and slipped a few of the larger nuggets into his pockets to serve as reminders of his good fortune on the long ride to Fort Benton.

Later that afternoon he came to a deep gulch with a cut bank and sides too steep to cross. He rode along the edge in search of a place where the banks had slumped or the entry of a side channel with gentler slopes. No such place appeared, forcing Daniel to travel well to the north of his intended path. While he reconnoitered along the edge of the gulch, the bottom remained invisible unless he looked down from its very edge. Eventually, however, he came to a bend with a view straight along the bottom of the channel. Here a chilling scene came into view. Almost immediately below him but separated by a ten-foot bank, a group of Blackfoot was busily slaughtering a cow. The men were bloody, their arms covered with it to their elbows, and their faces were streaked with a mixture of blood and sweat that glimmered in the stark light of the midday sun.

Stunned, Daniel simply stared down at the group before offering a greeting in English—an awkward attempt to communicate in a language none of the men understood. No one in the group responded, but one of the Blackfoot men reached for a rifle propped against the bank. A quick calculation convinced Daniel that his only option was to run. He turned his horse and raced across the open plains toward some badlands in the near distance, a place that might offer some cover. He made several hundred yards before he looked back and saw the Blackfoot emerge from the gulch.

Daniel's horsemanship was no match for the Blackfoot, who rapidly closed the distance as they raced across the open grassland, their bodies melded to their mounts. As the riders continued to gain, Daniel flailed the reins in a panicked attempt to increase his speed. His efforts were futile. As his arms tired, his grip weakened. A dip in the land and his horse's stagger were enough to throw him from the saddle. He hit the ground hard and stayed still for a moment, groggy but unhurt, breathing in the dust raised by his fall. As he lay there, slowly regaining his wits, he felt an odd detachment from the unfolding events. Instead his mind replayed a family story, one told throughout his youth with a currency that belied its origin nearly a hundred years before Daniel's birth. His great-grandfather, another Daniel, had served in the British army and had been wounded severely in one of the skirmishes leading up to the surrender at Yorktown. As he lay immobilized, a soldier from the other side approached, bayonet fixed, ready to skewer the elder Daniel. But the soldier paused, and his grim face briefly transformed into a grin that reflected his decision to leave the wounded man to his fate.

Daniel was still in his reverie when the Blackfoot arrived and brought their horses to a jarring stop. Secure in the knowledge that they could do anything they wanted with the helpless man lying before them, they stared at Daniel with a mixture of anger and curiosity. The Blackfoot again ignored Daniel's efforts to communicate in English and spoke only among themselves. Daniel understood not a word of their language, but it was obvious that they were discussing his fate.

Looks Beyond, the youngest of the three men, was the most agitated. He urged his companions to kill the white man who had come to this land uninvited and had wasted what he didn't own. "Our people will suffer this winter without the buffalo," said Looks Beyond. "This man, and the others like him, kill without need; they kill without hunger; and for this he should be the one who suffers."

The second man nodded, but the third man, Follows Bear, responded in a more measured tone. He somehow appeared dignified even with cow blood splattered on his face. "Looks Beyond sees much that is true," he acknowledged, "but we don't know what this man did, or who killed that buffalo. Killing this man will bring no honor. His death will only bring our people more trouble."

As the conversation continued, each man speaking more loudly and forcefully, Daniel sensed that his chances were fading quickly. Despite this, he maintained a serenity that made no sense under the circumstances but allowed him to think clearly. Finally, it occurred to him that these might be some of the "British Indians" who supposedly had crossed over from Canada. "Maybe they can speak French," he thought.

"Canada. Je suis Canadien," Daniel announced. A look of comprehension emerged from Follows Bear, who held up a hand to quiet the others. Daniel continued in French, "I don't give a damn about that cow. Take as many as you want. It's nothing to me, and I will say nothing of it."

These words bought Daniel more time. Follows Bear spoke enough French to understand Daniel's meaning, which prompted more discussion among the group.

Looks Beyond still urged the others to kill Daniel: "A desperate man will say anything to save his life. If we spare him, the lawmen will soon follow. Better to kill him now and leave his body where it won't be found."

As the discussion continued, Daniel thought of Jean Baptise and remembered his Blackfoot name and that he had many friends among the tribe. Hoping he had found the words that would save his life, he called out again: "I am a friend of LaValle, who was known by your people as Raven."

The name immediately elicited a look of recognition. Continuing to speak French, Daniel explained to Follows Bear, the apparent leader of the group, how he had met up with Jean Baptiste. Their conversation continued at length, prolonged by the need to translate for Follows Bear's companions, who listened intently but remained silent.

When they seemed to be finished with the news of LaValle, Looks Beyond pointed to Daniel and assumed a fiercer expression. He spoke angrily to Follows Bear, who then translated for Daniel: "Looks Beyond hates the white man for what has happened to the buffalo. He says the white man's buffalo are puny, they will die when the winter of many deaths returns and their rotting carcasses will blacken the land."[2] After a pause, Follows Bear added his own thoughts. "Each year we

---

[2] Looks Beyond's prophecy very nearly came true in the great die-off of the winter of 1886–1887.

see fewer buffalo. This year there were none all the way to the Big River. How could this be?"

Follows Bear paused again, as if he expected a response. Daniel was relieved when he pointed back toward the gulch and continued. "That cow was alone and strayed far from the herd. She would have been in a wolf's stomach before the sun was down."

Finally, with no indication that they were about to leave, the men rode off abruptly. Only Looks Beyond paused to look back. It was a close brush with death and Daniel slowly released his fear. To Looks Beyond it looked as if Daniel were grinning, and the Blackfoot man's anger deepened.

IX.

On a cool summer morning, Nellie and Helen boarded the stage to Fort Benton. The stage followed a well-worn road that took them almost straight north toward the Gates of the Mountains. As the distance from Helena increased, so did the two sisters' sense of freedom. They felt as if they were continuing the adventure they had begun in St. Louis. Enjoying the company of her fellow travelers, Nellie chatted almost nonstop and perhaps showed more enthusiasm among strangers than was proper for a young woman. But they all enjoyed it and Nellie's energetic conversation made the time pass quickly. By the time they reached Sun River, Nellie was exhausted. She drifted to sleep for much of the remainder of the trip.

The following day, Nellie awoke in the front bedroom of her aunt's house. The room faced the river and its steep gray bluffs loomed above it like battlement walls. The filtered light of morning hid the rough edges of town and illuminated the cottonwoods along the river with a glow, adding their reflection to the already silvery water. Enchanted by the scene, Nellie quickly dressed to go outside and take it all in. She had hardly seen Fort Benton upon her arrival on the *Red Cloud* and was eager to immerse herself in this new setting, which offered both a chance to see Daniel again and freedom from the confines of her father's supervision.

Helen was already on the front porch and greeted her sister with a sweep of her arms. "Well, Nellie, here we are. How do you propose to find this Daniel of yours?"

"There aren't that many places to look, Helen. Let's just treat these days like a holiday and stroll the town at our leisure. Aunt Betsy said the boat traffic has already dropped off, so there's not much going on. If he's here, we'll find each other."

In 1882 Fort Benton was in the midst of a building boom. On that day, workmen were putting the finishing touches on the towering façade of the Grand Union Hotel. Nellie and Helen stopped to observe the work more closely. From the scaffolds hanging from the building, they heard a voice, or maybe a soft whistle. Helen insisted they move on. But Nellie called up in the direction of the sound, "Does anyone here know a Daniel McHarg?"

In an instant, one of the men rappelled down the building and walked over to them. Helen was now truly appalled and insisted that they move on. She started walking away, but Nellie stood her ground and introduced herself as well as her sister, who reluctantly stopped and turned back to join them.

"Pleased to meet you, ladies," said the worker. "I'm John Campbell. I came upriver on the *Red Cloud* and spent a lot of time with Daniel. He went to look for gold and no one's seen him here for a few weeks."

Nellie pulled out a clipping from the *River Press* and read the article about the tragedy that had befallen Limestone. "Look," she said, pointing, "it also says that Daniel intended to return to Fort Benton. Shouldn't he be here by now?"

Helen and even Nellie now feared that the conversation could get awkward. Nellie didn't want to appear too eager or to answer any inquiries about why she was looking for Daniel. "When you see Daniel, please give him my condolences," she said.

John agreed to do so and Nellie turned abruptly to leave, closely followed by Helen who quietly fumed at her sister's indiscretion and the embarrassment she felt it brought to them both.

X.

Upon arising early, Daniel was relieved to see that the heavy rain that had awakened him near midnight had stopped. He was cheered by the thought that he'd make it back to Fort Benton today. The country remained open prairie, broken here and there by a coulee or a low butte. With little to observe and lulled by the steady movement of his horse, Daniel's mind drifted and his thoughts turned to Nellie. In his mind she always appeared just as she had that day they'd talked on the river, her long skirt rippling from the vigor of her movement as she walked back to the boat, her white blouse tightly buttoned around her neck.

As Daniel approached the rim of a minor coulee, the sudden movement of a man standing up shattered this pleasant image. Looks Beyond had been observing Daniel from a distance for much of the morning. He was waiting for the right time to kill a man who symbolized all that had become wrong in his rapidly changing world. Daniel had a sickening recognition that this was the man he had come to fear. Before Daniel could move, Looks Beyond dropped him with a single shot to the torso. He then walked up and looked at Daniel closely, satisfied that the wound would be mortal and that without any assistance likely he would die a slow, lingering death. While telling Daniel that such a death would be his fate, Looks Beyond took Daniel's rifle and the small box in his saddlebag. He left behind the horse, which bore a prominent brand and thus brought with it the likelihood of troubling questions should he encounter anyone from the white man's government.

Daniel lay sprawled on the grass, his blood staining the ground, for most of the day. He couldn't have known for how long, for he was unconscious much of the time, but he later remembered how dried out he felt and how he had dreamed of lying in a forest with a soft mist in the air. While having this dream, Daniel felt the presence of someone. It turned out to be Jean Baptiste.

Follows Bear had visited Jean Baptiste the day after his encounter with Daniel. He had told LaValle about Looks

Beyond's anger and about how he had left his fellow tribesmen the previous night. Follows Bear shared his concern that Looks Beyond would pursue Daniel. Jean Baptiste was certain of it and set out to find Daniel immediately.

The trail was easy to follow, and LaValle found Daniel lying in the coarse short grass, his location marked by the horse that remained by his side. After peeling away Daniel's bloody shirt, Jean Baptiste saw that it was a bad wound. He turned Daniel over to see if the bullet had exited, but it remained buried deep in his body.

Jean Baptiste was a surgeon of sorts. He had sewn up men and had treated the stabbings, shootings, and other mishaps that could befall a man on the frontier. He had even sewn himself up on more than one occasion. But Daniel's wound was one of the worst he'd seen, and he knew he had to remove the bullet quickly and stop the bleeding. He arranged the tools he needed for the job and began with an abundant dousing of whiskey, which caused Daniel to stir and to moan in pain. Before starting to probe, Jean Baptiste spoke: "Daniel, if you can hear me, just know this. You have to want to live. I can't help you without that."

It was a difficult process, but after an hour he was finished. Satisfied he had done his best, Jean Baptiste drank deeply from the whiskey jug and set himself up for what would likely be a long wait.

By the third day, Daniel had stirred but had developed a fever. Jean Baptiste made a yarrow tea to keep the fever in check and hoped that Daniel had the strength he'd need to survive. More days passed, and though Daniel grew more alert, he remained quiet, almost solemn, due not only to the physical toll the wound had taken, but also from a feeling that something even more important than Limestone's gold had been lost.

Jean Baptiste didn't mind the quiet as he busied himself with Daniel's care. Nor did the quiet stop *him* from talking. Indeed, this was the kind of conversation Jean Baptiste enjoyed most. He could talk of any subject he liked while Daniel just listened, an occasional nod providing the only acknowledgment Jean Baptiste needed to keep going. For LaValle it was certainly better than talking to himself or to his dogs, something he did with regularity when holed up in his cabin in the depths of winter.

Jean Baptiste made an occasional foray away from their camp in order to replenish their meat supply, but he usually returned empty-handed because most of the game were in the high country at that time of year and he didn't want to leave Daniel alone for long. After returning one evening, Jean Baptiste reported to Daniel that he had seen a grizzly bear not far from their camp. "It's a good sign for you, Daniel. The Blackfoot believe grizzlies have a powerful spirit." He then launched into a long story about the time a Blackfoot warrior was wounded in a battle with the Snakes. As he lay alone and slowly dying, the warrior prayed for survival and was rescued by a bear, who placed a healing mud on his wounds and carried him back to his people. Jean Baptiste concluded, "I am like the bear, Daniel. I can be cranky and sometimes need to withdraw like bears need to hibernate. But my medicine is also strong. Ha! Is it not so, my friend?"

Daniel still didn't feel like talking much—the effort brought pain to his chest. But he couldn't resist responding. "That's a good comparison, Jean Baptiste. Especially the cranky part. Maybe the hairy part as well."

Jean Baptiste was in good spirits that day and mimicked the movements of a bear, swaying from side to side and laughing heartily. He was happy to see the hint of a smile in Daniel's expression before Daniel tilted his hat down over his face to resume his rest.

After another week, Jean Baptiste declared that Daniel was ready to travel and they started toward Fort Benton. They went slowly, taking days to complete a trip that normally would have been much faster. Upon reaching the bluffs above the Missouri River, Daniel paused to look down on Benton. The town seemed larger than he remembered.

Despite Daniel's urging, Jean Baptiste was determined to go no farther. Thoughts of a crowded town and the barrage of questions that would follow their arrival were more than he could bear. Sensing Daniel's disappointment, Jean Baptiste quipped that the company of a whore had been one of the few things that could bring him into a town—but now he was too old to be tempted even by that. They parted with the awkwardness a man feels when he has received a gift that can't be repaid properly. Jean Baptiste muttered something about having done it for Limestone, but he later regretted those words, for he had come to like Daniel and feared his words would diminish a bond that had become important to him.

XI.

Daniel was still weak, and he lay low for a few days before venturing into the town. His first foray was to a store that also served as an assay office. The few gold nuggets he had kept in his pocket replenished his diminishing stake and left him with enough cash to get by for a while without having to work the long hours of a carpenter in summer.

Word that someone had cashed in a few large nuggets moved quickly through town. The assay clerk reported that the man was a Canadian who claimed to have found the nuggets near Maiden. The small-town rumor trail led straight to Daniel, who suddenly found his boarding room filled with visitors, including John Campbell and another passenger from the *Red Cloud.* Daniel wasn't in the mood for company, but his friends were eager to see him.

John was especially excited because he had something to show Daniel. "I hope you found some gold, Daniel," he said, "or your admirers back in Minnesota will be disappointed." John read from a neatly folded clipping from the *Montevideo Leader,* which had been republished in the Fort Benton newspaper:

> *We acknowledge the receipt from Daniel McHarg, formerly of this place but now in Benton, Mont., of an interesting edition of the* River Press*, , published at that place. Judging from the evidence of thrift and prosperity in the* Press*, we think Benton is bound to boom, and we hope Daniel will boom with it and come back with his pockets full of rock.*

Daniel had forgotten that he'd sent a letter, along with a few articles from the *River Press*, to a newspaperman who had become a good friend during his years in Minnesota.

"So let's have it, Daniel," John continued. "Do you have any more rocks in those pockets of yours?"

It was good for a laugh, but they were genuine in inquiring about Daniel's health. They wanted to hear all about how he had been shot and how he had managed such a heroic escape.

"I didn't do a damn thing," Daniel said. The comment came across abruptly and without his usual humor. "If it hadn't been for an old trapper, I'd be lying there now."

John decided not to press. Remembering that he had some other news for Daniel, he changed the subject again. "I saw that Nellie of yours, she and her sister. They asked about you and seemed pretty embarrassed to be seen showing an interest in a rambler like you."

Daniel wanted to know all the details, especially whether Nellie was still in town and where he might find her.

"I don't know where she's staying," John replied, "but after we saw her at the hotel she and her sister headed toward the nice homes further up Front Street."

Not long after receiving that information, Daniel thanked his friends for coming by and sent them on their way with the promise that he'd be better company soon enough.

The next day, after a late breakfast, Daniel tidied himself up and put on a new shirt he had hurriedly purchased at Gans & Klein, a store that sold finer goods than he typically bought. There weren't many homes on Front Street above the commercial district, so his task wasn't hopeless. He knocked on a few doors and inquired about Nellie until a woman directed him to a yellow house up the street. Before he got there, he saw Nellie and her sister sitting on the porch—a marvelous sight for a man who had begun to worry his life would unravel again. Nellie tried to exercise restraint but couldn't suppress the sweet smile Daniel remembered. She sent Helen inside to tell Aunt Betsy that the man was someone she knew.

Daniel was thinner than Nellie remembered, so that's how their conversation started. "Mr. McHarg," she quipped, "are you too busy looking for gold to take time to eat?"

Nellie followed up with an offer to serve Daniel some breakfast, but he declined, wanting nothing to interfere with such a long-awaited moment. Yet they hardly knew each other, and the intensity of their feelings was wildly disproportionate to the amount of time they had actually spent together. It wasn't easy to manage the conversation under these circumstances. They had much information to share, but neither was comfortable expressing the powerful feelings that mattered most: that they had thought of each other continuously and that something had been missing in their lives from the moment they had separated. That acknowledgement would come later.

For now, they stuck to the events. Daniel's account of his near-death experience was a shock. Nellie almost couldn't bear to hear it, even though Daniel, thinner but otherwise appearing well, was sitting right next to her. They talked for almost an hour, after which Daniel left, reluctant yet elated by Nellie's insistence that he return the next day for a noon meal. Though an unfortunate turn of events, Daniel's wound turned out to be an opportunity for the hopeful couple, as none of the Sage women could doubt the propriety of helping someone— even a near stranger—regain his health. Nellie would make the most of this opportunity.

As Nellie expected, Aunt Betsy agreed that Daniel would be welcome to eat with the family, thus beginning a routine that brought him to the house for a noon meal most days for the next few weeks. The three women shared in the cooking. The knowledge that they were helping someone recover from a serious wound made their efforts purposeful, and all three enjoyed Daniel's company. After Nellie's aunt came to know Daniel better, other possibilities for Nellie and Daniel to spend time together emerged. They took long walks through the town or just sat by the river. Helen usually joined them, but she made sure they also had time alone.

As summer waned and the days grew noticeably shorter, Daniel could feel himself recovering, not only because of the pounds he had gained, but also because of a lessening of the darkness that had crept back into his soul after he had been shot. Though he began to laugh more easily and to feel joy in Nellie's presence, sometimes a shadow would return while he was alone in the night. At those moments, Daniel couldn't help but feel a sense of futility and doubt in himself. He told himself that he was foolish to believe he could shed the burden of a tragic loss and build a new life with the stability and prosperity that a woman like Nellie should expect. With a concentrated effort, he could still push these dark thoughts away.

At the end of August, it was time for Nellie to return to Helena. Helen needed to start the school year and they had stayed in Fort Benton for as long as they could. In the times they had enjoyed alone and focused only on each other, Daniel and Nellie had begun to talk of a future together. At first, Daniel was reluctant to share much of his life in New Brunswick, as he feared his tragic past would push Nellie away. Nellie cried when he finally told her of his loss, but the news had an effect opposite to what he expected. Nellie now knew that Daniel's real healing would be more complicated; it would take longer than his recovery from a gunshot wound. She wasn't a woman easily deterred, and her deepening love for Daniel would not be an exception.

Their talk of a future life was tentative at first, but it grew to include settling on some land along the Teton River. Daniel would begin the process of claiming the land and then go to Helena, where the government land office was located, and buy 160 acres through an exemption claim. It would take some time to perfect the claim, improvements had to be made on the land. But when the work was done he would come to Helena and ask Nellie's father for his approval to marry her.

After Nellie left for Helena, Daniel got right to work. He spent a few nights camping along the Teton and walked and rode the land for several days before selecting an acreage that consisted almost entirely of bottom land, with an abundance of trees and ground that could be tilled for grain crops or hay. Although the parcel was far too small to support a cattle ranch, these 160 acres would be the home place, a haven set amid grasslands that stretched to the horizon, unfenced and still available for the taking by those with the courage and determination to turn cattle loose on a range where wolves, blizzards, and thieves were constant threats.

Later that fall, when he felt fully recovered, Daniel began the difficult work of making the needed improvements to the land, including breaking some of the ground and building fencing, corrals, and the beginnings of a house. He did much of the work himself, though he occasionally recruited John Campbell and a few other friends to help.

Before winter settled in, Daniel made a trip to the Judith River. He took along some buffalo meat for Jean Baptiste, who prepared a feast that lasted long into the night. Jean Baptiste was glad for the company, but he complained bitterly of the slow toll that age was taking on his body. "Daniel," he said, "I could once live on gristle and walk for days with a load that would make a mule balk. But now I have days when it's almost too much to do the simple things one must do to live."

Though Daniel pressed, Jean Baptiste offered no particulars on his condition. He asserted that he felt good today and that was all that mattered. Daniel told LaValle of his place on the Teton and his plans to marry and to get into the cattle business. LaValle was delighted to hear of Daniel's marriage plans but he couldn't understand his ambition to start a ranch. He believed that cattle didn't belong in Montana and that attempts to replace the buffalo made no sense. But LaValle held his tongue on the matter and instead told Daniel about a time when a Crow raiding party ambushed a group of Blackfoot very close to where Daniel was building his house. "If you hear a sound in the night like the moan of a dying man, my friend, it will be the Blackfoot," said Jean Baptiste.

Daniel grew alarmed. He was only partly reassured when Jean Baptiste told him that these Blackfoot were only lost souls and meant no harm.

XII.

That winter was the longest in Nellie's life. Though she and Daniel wrote often, she felt isolated from all that had become important to her, including the new friends she had made in Fort Benton. Matters were made worse by an ongoing conflict with her father, who not only tried to control Nellie's activities but also seemed to disagree with her on nearly every issue she held important. At the dinner table the conversation inevitably became argumentative, despite Mrs. Sage's gentle efforts to intercede. Mr. Sage, whose position as the owner of a major mine gave him immediate entry into Helena's emerging elite, was used to deference, particularly from the women in his own household. He found it difficult to accept any questioning of his firmly held beliefs, which nearly all his peers shared. These beliefs revolved around a sort of manifest destiny, with respect not only to Indian lands and resources but also to the relationship between labor and management, as well as men and women and their right to vote.

One evening, after an especially vehement disagreement about the treatment of miners and their families, Mr. Sage decided to try harder to modify Nellie's views by providing her with a glimpse of the miner's world. He thought he'd be able to demonstrate that the miners were content—happy to have a job and the ability to support their families. Mr. Sage claimed that the miners and their managers were engaged in a mutually beneficial arrangement that represented an improvement to the conditions that many of the foreigners in the workforce had left behind in their native lands.

Mr. Sage had another motive driving his plan, however. He wanted to introduce Nellie to a young man who worked at his mine as a clerk, someone Mr. Sage felt had better prospects than Daniel did. Though Daniel and Mr. Sage hadn't met, Nellie's description of Daniel provided Mr. Sage with little confidence that the young man was up to the job of supporting his eldest daughter. Mr. Sage thought that Daniel's proposed ranch would amount to nothing, and that the emerging cattle industry would be controlled by those backed with big capital behind them—such as the D-S Ranch that was building a herd of more than ten thousand head in the Judith Basin. Without the backing of the money men, Mr. Sage asserted, Daniel was destined for a life spent dirt-poor and an early grave. Mr. Sage implied to Nellie that he might be able to offer assistance to Daniel, but she knew Daniel would want no part of it, and this only made Mr. Sage less supportive of the relationship.

The next day, as Nellie had reluctantly agreed, they set off for the mine, which required a long carriage ride from Helena. The distance was great enough that Mr. Sage occasionally spent a few nights at the mine site, but the prospect of living in a mining camp had little appeal compared to the elegance of Helena. Father and daughter both knew that the ride would seem even longer if the conversation became unpleasant, so they kept things light, limiting their comments to the scenery they passed through and their mutual excitement about the prospect of rail service arriving the following year.

After the carriage ascended through a narrow canyon, the mine came into view. They were greeted by the clerk Mr. Sage was eager to introduce to Nellie. The clerk was a charmer who focused his attention on Nellie immediately. He told her how much he had heard about her musical talents and made other flattering references to her appearance, telling her that she was even more beautiful than her father had indicated. Nellie remained polite, but she found the exchange distasteful.

Following this brief encounter, the usual tension between Nellie and her father returned. Mr. Sage described the clerk as a brilliant young man who would go far. "You ought to get to know him better, Nellie," he said.

Mr. Sage's comment set Nellie off. She not only found the clerk unappealing, but also resented her father's implication that she was open to meeting other men after she had told him of the seriousness of her feelings toward Daniel. "Father," she said, "you ought to know me better than to think that an obsequious clerk of yours is someone I'd find interesting." This remark set the tone for what was to come.

They had timed their arrival to observe the end of a shift, when the miners emerged from the depths, happy to see the light of day again. The men were accustomed to seeing Mr. Sage about the mine property; he made a habit of engaging in small talk with them and seemed to enjoy the interplay with his workers. This was what Mr. Sage had brought Nellie to see. He hoped that the good cheer he could usually elicit from the men would demonstrate that the workers didn't view him as some sort of a demon and that they maintained their dignity and a degree of joviality despite the hard work and risks their jobs demanded.

At first all went according to Mr. Sage's plan. He cheerfully interacted with the men and promised each a holiday treat at Christmas, which was just weeks away. Nellie observed her father's demonstration and noted a certain amount of goodwill. However, she felt certain that he had staged it all for her benefit. And after several of the men had passed, her attention was drawn to a young man—a boy, really—who had been crippled by an accident in the mine and could no longer work. He supported himself with a pair of homemade crutches. Because the young man had little to do with his time, and because he knew that the miners sometimes shared leftover food from their pails, he often appeared at shift changes. On occasion the miners even slipped him a coin or two to supplement the meager settlement he had received from the company as compensation for his injury.

After seeing one of the miners hand the young man a bit of food, Nellie walked over to him. Her father observed this action as he continued greeting the workers, determined to stay until the last one had passed.

"Forgive my directness," Nellie said to the young man, "but what happened to your leg? Will it heal?"

"No, ma'am. A whole pile of rocks fell on my leg. It was a bad break, and the bone didn't get set well. I guess the doc might have been drunk." He laughed and added, "I did get a hundred dollars from the company. It won't last long, but I guess I knew what I was getting myself into when I signed on to be a miner."

Just then Mr. Sage stepped in. He flashed a smile toward the injured miner, who now felt awkward and a little nervous in the presence of the powerful mine owner.

Looking around to see who was observing, Mr. Sage spoke loudly. "See, Nellie, the miners take care of their own. We've certainly done our part as his employer, more than what we're required to do by the law."

Nellie felt an emerging rage. "This young man's plight is tragic," she said to her father. "A hundred-dollar settlement is ridiculous. Do you not see the injustice in this?"

Mr. Sage quickly pointed out that the company had offered the standard settlement in the young man's case, and he couldn't pay every injured man a fortune without going broke. Certain that she had already caused enough of a scene, Nellie ignored her father. Before bolting back to the carriage, however, she handed the crippled man what little money she had in her bag. Several of the miners witnessed her act.

The ride back to Helena proceeded in silence. Mr. Sage was also furious. He was uncertain as to how the men would react to the drama Nellie had created and what he should do to correct it. Just before they reached the edge of town, Mr. Sage told Nellie that he had made a decision. Nellie would have to return with him to the mine on another day and act decently, in order to show the men that her behavior today was an aberration and that the family was unified. Nellie immediately refused, which caused her father to issue an ultimatum: either she agree—and, more broadly, show him more respect—or she'd no longer be welcome in his household.

The next day at breakfast, Nellie calmly announced that she was leaving. She planned to take a room of her own and to support herself with her small savings and her earnings from teaching piano. It would be enough, she thought, to sustain her until the time when she and Daniel would be married. Her mother begged her to reconsider, while her father stoically sat in silence, perhaps more upset by the loss of control over his family than by his daughter's departure.

Looking back later on, Nellie viewed her months living alone in Helena as a turning point in her life. She realized then that she could make a life on her own. She also learned how rewarding it was to help others, a practice perhaps motivated by her encounter with the crippled miner. In addition to working as a piano teacher that winter, Nellie found time to volunteer at a hospital serving the poor.

XIII.

In June, Daniel and Nellie were married in Helena in a small ceremony attended by only a few close friends. Mr. Sage did not attend, and he forbade his family to attend as well. Daniel and Nellie returned to Fort Benton the next day and spent one night in the Grand Union Hotel before heading out to their home on the Teton. Their return prompted a short piece in the *River Press*:

*Daniel McHarg and Miss Nellie Sage were
married in Helena Sunday evening, and
Daniel brought his bride home last night.
Mr. McHarg is well known and universally
popular in Benton and we believe his
young wife will never have cause to regret
the trust she reposed in him. Mrs. McHarg
resided in Benton some time last year,
where she made many friends who will
give her a warm welcome back. The
happy couple are comfortably housed in
their new home on the Teton, and <u>River
Press</u> joins with their friends in wishes for
a happy life.*

The newlyweds rode to their place on the Teton on a
glorious day when the grass retained a spring green
and the river sparkled under a cloudless sky. Nellie
found the setting enchanting but flinched when she saw
the building that would become their home. In his
letters earlier that year Daniel had tried to prepare her
for the fact that the house was a simple affair and that
he'd make improvements over time. But the undeniable
fact remained that it was plain, small, and consisted of
just two rooms. Nonetheless, Nellie was happy just to
be with Daniel, and she told him it was lovely.

"Daniel, you've outdone yourself," she proclaimed with
humor in her tone. "But tell me, where will the servants'
quarters be?"

Daniel put on a formal manner, ushered her through the
front door, and pointed to the new wing he was
planning as she pushed him onto a rickety bed, their
laughter filling the small space inside the building's four
rough walls.

There was still much work to do. Nellie focused on making a home of their "shanty on the prairie" while Daniel divided his time between buying and managing livestock, making improvements to their property, and occasionally working in town for a little extra income.

As evening approached one August day, when the summer was overripe and any hint of lushness had vanished from the land, Daniel and Nellie rewarded themselves with some rest. They sat in the shade by their house and gazed toward the river and the rounded bluffs just beyond. At this time of day they often spotted deer tucked in to the folds of the land, and this was their first thought when a figure appeared at the top of a ridge.

For a moment the figure remained motionless, silhouetted against a towering sky. Then it moved, initially with only a slow wave of one arm, followed by a slow advance down the slope. It was a horseman, soon revealed to be an Indian. He seemed to be traveling alone, but they couldn't be sure. As the figure approached the house, Daniel went for his rifle and urged Nellie to go inside. She refused, stating that whatever danger they may face, they would face it together. There wasn't enough time to argue, for the horseman had picked up the pace and was within hailing distance. Daniel heard the man yell out, "Hey, Canada! Canada!"

The man was backlit by the lowering sun, making it difficult to see his features, so Daniel didn't know immediately who it was; he was only certain that it was an Indian. But the voice was familiar and brought back a painful memory. Even if the man wasn't Looks

Beyond, Daniel had no reason to be comfortable with any of the Blackfoot men he had encountered that day. Once again Daniel silently urged Nellie to go inside, but she continued to resist, gently pushing away the hand he pressed against her hip. Daniel started to speak to the man in English but was interrupted by a request, spoken with a surprising politeness:

"Francais, s'il vous plait. Parlez francais."

Daniel shouted back, in French, "I think I remember you, but hold there until I can figure it out for sure."

The man stopped his advance. "Jean Baptiste sent me. There is no other reason I would be here. He asked me to do something for him. So I am here."

"Why would Jean Baptiste send you here?"

In response, the man reached for something. It was a small box with the distinctive markings that were on the gift Daniel had received from Limestone. Daniel loosened his tight grip on the rifle and urged the man to come ahead. It was Follows Bear, who reported, "Looks Beyond is dead. The whiskey got him, and they killed him for his gold—the gold he took from you." Then Follows Bear threw the box to the ground near Daniel, which opened when it hit, spilling its contents into the grass. Looks Beyond had left the box and the meager amount of gold it still contained with his family before heading off in search of whiskey. It was all that remained of Limestone's gold.

"Who killed him," Daniel asked, "and where did it happen?"

Follows Bear explained that the killers had been white men—the worst kind of white men. "There's a place just off the reservation called Wolf Hole. Looks Beyond went there in search of whiskey. It's an evil place."

Daniel had heard of the place and knew that cattle thieves and other outlaws congregated there. Apparently it was a place that attracted the worst among men, a place where death was often just an argument away or merely another man's amusement. Still, Daniel wanted to know more. "Why was he killed? Did he cause any trouble?"

Follows Bear had gone to Wolf Hole himself after Looks Beyond had failed to return. One of the white men there reported that Looks Beyond had been shot for his gold and thrown in a gully. Follows Bear had retrieved what was left of the body and would carry the painful memory of that day until his own death. He never answered Daniel's question directly. He simply said, "Looks Beyond was sick in his heart. His anger at things he couldn't change made him sick, and the whiskey only made it worse. It was the same anger that made him shoot you."

Daniel was unsure what to do next, but Nellie quickly stepped in, thanking Follows Bear and urging him to come into the house. He refused but clearly appreciated the gesture. Then he turned his horse and trotted off.

XIV.

Daniel had named their place Raven Ranch, a slightly mocking tribute to Jean Baptiste, who had no use for cattle but had been given that name by the Blackfoot. Daniel continued to divide his time between work on the ranch and a job in town. On some days Nellie would accompany him to Fort Benton, where she visited Aunt Betsy and supplemented their income by teaching piano. By the following spring they had settled into an almost comfortable routine, but their goal of building a successful cattle business remained elusive. The coming of the northern railroad was still a few years off, and the local market remained small. Daniel found a few places to sell the beef they raised, but without the income they earned in town they wouldn't have made it.

That summer, on a day when the work on one of the new buildings in town had been particularly hard, Daniel felt worn out. He had shrugged off prior invitations to join the boys for a drink, but his resistance wavered that day. For the remainder of that summer, a stop at the saloon became part of his routine. On some nights Daniel didn't make it back to the Teton until near dark, and he often faded into a deep sleep shortly after his return. At first Nellie accepted his behavior in the hope that it was temporary, but it became a source of conflict, which escalated after a night when Daniel failed to return at all. He arrived the following morning with his clothes dusty and adorned with bits of dried grass picked up from a night sleeping on the hard prairie ground.

That morning Daniel felt Nellie's wrath, which she delivered quietly and without drama. "Daniel," she said, "I won't be treated this way. I can't live with a man who cares so little for his marriage, and if you don't stop it immediately, I'm going back to Helena."

She was right, he knew, and any resistance he might have felt withered in the presence of her determined stare. Daniel apologized and promised he would change.

Nellie softened a bit and continued, "Daniel, do you really know what it means to love someone? It's not about needing someone, or about feelings. It's knowing that when you're together your life has more meaning, that together you're each a better person than you are alone. I want us to always believe that."

From that point on, whenever Daniel worked in town, he returned home promptly. John Campbell and the others understood what had to be done, but they laughed a little less when Daniel was gone.

Although he often spent more time with a hammer in his hand than working the land, Daniel remained optimistic about the future of the cattle industry in Montana and slowly built up a small herd. His optimism was challenged that winter when he went out to check on his animals and found the remains of several lying dead, their blood vividly staining the snow. One animal was still alive, its entrails hanging from a stomach that had been torn open by wolves. Daniel could barely stand the horrible sound of its pathetic cries. He dispatched the animal with a shot from his rifle, but the experience wasn't easily forgotten.

The next day, Daniel went to town and stopped at one of the saloons. It was early in the day, but he needed something to take his mind off the image of slaughter that hung hard in his memory. He hadn't been there long when an acquaintance, one of the old-timers who had been in Montana since the early days, said that he had been by Jean Baptiste's place a few days earlier and that LaValle had asked for Daniel.

"How is the old hermit?" Daniel asked, and added that Jean Baptiste had saved his life and was one of the few men he'd walk into hell to assist.

"Daniel, the man is fading. I don't think he's got much longer."

The winter had been relatively mild, and Daniel immediately determined that he had to go to Jean Baptiste's cabin on the Judith. He first went home to tell Nellie of his plans and to gather a few items he'd need to make the trip. She was frightened by the prospect of his traveling so far alone in winter and tried to deter him. She also knew that Daniel could be stubborn about certain things, and this seemed to be one of them. He rode off late that afternoon, on a day when the sun shone only periodically but the snow cover was thin and in many places it had blown clear and exposed the ground. He spent the first night camped in the open.

The weather on the following day was much like the day before and Daniel made good time along the stage road. As the afternoon faded toward darkness, the clouds began to thicken and a few snowflakes could be seen falling slowly and drifting along with a light wind. By the time Daniel was just north of Grizzly Butte, the intensity of the snowfall had increased, something he sensed more by its soft touch on his face than by what he could see in the mounting darkness. Though eager to make it as far as possible that day, he decided to spend the night at the stage stop, where he was warmly greeted by Anna, the German woman who remembered his group and the lovely sound of the violin his fellow passenger had played that day. Despite the apparent lack of warmth in her relationship with Limestone, she expressed sadness at the news of his death and marked the occasion with a toast to his memory.

XV.

The next day Daniel awoke early. A light snow continued to fall, but little had accumulated. Anna urged Daniel to delay his trip. "Stay here for a while, Daniel," she said. "Why take a chance with the storm? You know how things can change so quickly. This can be a very cruel place."

Daniel knew that, but it wasn't far now to the Judith. He brushed her concerns aside with "I'll be fine, Mutter," prompting Anna to throw a bit of bread at him. It bounced off his forehead and landed in his coffee, and they both laughed like silly children. Still, Anna was concerned when Daniel left, and she watched him until he disappeared from sight.

After crossing Arrow Creek and ascending onto the bench, Daniel left the stage road and headed to the northeast, instead following a route that would take him directly to Jean Baptiste's place. He had about twenty more miles to cover. The wind had started to blow harder, and snow had accumulated in several of the coulees, so his pace slowed. But most worrisome was the fact that the snow was now falling heavily. Each mile became more difficult as the snow deepened. It had also become bitterly cold.

By the time LaValle's cabin first came into view, still a half mile distant, it was near dark. Daniel was now cold and exhausted. As he approached more closely, he could see that there was no light inside the cabin and no smoke emerged from the chimney. It was a dreadful sight, leaving Daniel with only the hope that Jean Baptiste had left. But it was a desperate hope, for it didn't fit with what he had come to know of how the man lived.

There was no response when Daniel pounded on the door, which opened with a lift of the latch. Jean Baptiste was at home. He sat dead in his chair by the fireplace, his body locked in a grotesque pose. Daniel looked closely at his friend, held his twisted fingers, and slumped into a chair next to him. A jug of whiskey sat nearby. The cheap liquor burned his throat, nearly choking him at first but then soothed his exhaustion. He drank heavily from the jug and began a conversation with Jean Baptiste, one that ended as Daniel slid into the frozen embrace of the long winter night.

XVI.

Nellie had planned to wait at home until Daniel returned, but on the second day she couldn't bear to be there alone any longer. In the fading light of the afternoon, as a light snow fell, she rode to her aunt's house in town. Then, assuring her aunt that she'd be back soon, she went to learn what she could about the weather—and, hopefully, about Daniel's whereabouts, even if only a report from someone who might have passed him on the stage road.

Nellie knew that John Campbell and his friends still gathered at the Antlers almost nightly. She headed there directly and hesitated only briefly before pushing open the door. It was now full dark, and the interior of the saloon was dimly lit by a few kerosene lanterns, each casting an amber light that softened the edges of the room and the faces of the men inside. She entered the room slowly and stood there for a moment, with the hope that someone would noticed her before she had to penetrate the inner sanctum of a place where women rarely ventured, certainly not alone, and not if they feared for their reputations. But she wasn't noticed immediately, and after standing still for a few awkward moments, she continued her approach towards the bar. Before she fully made her way across the room, her presence elicited a comment from one of the men.

"Boys, we have a visitor!" a man loudly exclaimed.

Nellie moved forward slowly, dreading the thought of finding herself in a room full of only strangers who would have thought her reckless or worse. She was greatly relieved when she heard John Campbell call her name, followed by a warning to his peers: "Gentlemen, this is Daniel's wife, and if any man says anything unkind, he'll have to deal with me." John ushered Nellie to a corner of the room, and his tone became more direct. "Nellie, what are you doing here? Daniel would be shocked and angry as hell to know about this."

Nellie told John of Daniel's departure for LaValle's place. "I'm worried, John," she said. "He's made this trip before, but not in winter."

John apologized for his harsh words and tried to reassure her. "Daniel knows that country, Nellie. He can take care of himself."

Nellie remained less than reassured. "Has anyone come in from the Judith country today?" she asked. "What's the weather there?" She noticed John hesitate and urged him further, "Please, John, what have you heard?"

John replied directly. "A stage driver came in from the Judith earlier today, Nellie. He claimed it was snowing hard and beginning to blow there." John regretted his honesty after seeing Nellie's worried look intensify. "If Daniel's not back tomorrow," he said, "I'll go look for him myself."

Nellie thanked him and spent a restless night at her aunt's house, waking once to a dream of Daniel alone in a vast and frozen landscape.

XVII.

Some say the temperature reached thirty below that night; others reported minus forty. The wind blew hard throughout the night, drifting snow into impassable barriers that trapped wildlife and cattle alike, randomly coating trees and other objects with ice, and creating a deathly beauty not fully revealed until the sun rose the following day. It blew hard enough to open the door to Jean Baptiste's cabin, though perhaps Daniel hadn't latched it properly. In any event, Daniel awoke that morning covered in snow, his eyes coated with a thin layer of ice that made them difficult to open.

His first thought that day was that he must be dead. He felt trapped in a body that didn't want to move and eyes that couldn't see. After slowly becoming aware of his surroundings, he was struck by a sudden fear that he might be frozen for good. His initial efforts to move his limbs failed, and his mind began to race, bringing thoughts of a worried Nellie, concerns about his cattle, and an appreciation of the irony of freezing to death when all his Baptist fears had been built on images of lost souls burning in hell.

He thought of trying out another body part and called over to LaValle, "Jean Baptiste, why did you have to be such a goddamn hermit and live way out here in the middle of nothing?" That his voice still worked provided some assurance, but it also reminded him that his friend was dead—and that he would be too if he couldn't get control of himself.

With great effort Daniel crawled forward. His legs dragged behind him, but he felt some strength return in his arms. A kerosene lantern and some matches sat on a log by the hearth, and he was able to start a fire, which warmed him quickly. He was surprised that he began to shiver as his body warmed. This involuntary response loosened his limbs but brought a stinging pain to places where his skin had been exposed to the cold. Gradually his ability to move was restored, but he felt too weak to travel. Still, he had to fight a strong compulsion to set off for Fort Benton and relieve Nellie of the worry he was certain she felt.

There was a little lean-to where Jean Baptiste had sheltered his animals, and Daniel's horse had shown the good sense to lie in it that frigid night. She was still there when Daniel had recovered enough to look around outside of the cabin. He fed her a few handfuls of grain and gazed upon a wintry landscape with enough snow to make the going rough. Formidable drifts were scattered randomly where the unhindered wind had been free to play. "It's hopeless to go anywhere," Daniel thought as he squinted into the dazzling light of the reflecting sun.

That afternoon he busied himself with making a travois to haul Jean Baptiste's body into town. Even if Jean Baptiste would rather have been buried near his cabin, Daniel couldn't just leave his body there . . . and who knew when the ground would be soft enough to bury him properly? Later that evening, alone in the cabin with the ghostly presence of Jean Baptiste, Daniel warmed himself by the fire and fell fast asleep.

He awoke in the darkness of the winter night to the sounds of a strong wind, rattling objects outside and whistling through the chimney near where he lay. The racket was loud enough to motivate him to get up and peek out the door. The air was surprisingly warm, enough so that water had begun dripping off the roof. Daniel had heard of a warm wind called a Chinook, but he had never experienced the phenomenon. He settled back into his bedding with the hope that he'd be able to travel sooner than he had thought possible earlier that day.

By sunup, the Chinook had done its work. The warm air it brought had tamed the snow and diminished the barrier drifts that had so recently loomed around the cabin. Though only a temporary reprieve from winter, Chinooks were not unusual in Montana, where temperature increases of fifty degrees or more have been recorded, sometimes occurring within a matter of hours.

This was the window Daniel needed. He set off that morning once the sun was full up, Jean Baptist bouncing along behind him. Still, it wasn't easy going, and the ordeal of the past few days had weakened Daniel. By late afternoon, he had only made it back to the stage station, where he arrived looking worn out and a bit unsteady on his feet. Anna, who had begun to worry about Daniel after the storm had intensified, chided him for not heeding her warnings. Daniel shrugged off her scolding with a comment that he'd drunk enough whiskey over the years to keep him from freezing. "Most of us Canadians are partially pickled, Anna. We might get cold and stiff, but we just don't freeze to death."

Despite her concern over Daniel's condition, Anna laughed heartily. Then things got serious. Daniel told her how badly he felt about putting so much worry on his wife, a kind of fear Anna knew about first hand. He also told her that he couldn't stay long and had to get back to Fort Benton that night and let Nellie know that he was alright.

"Daniel, you need some rest", Anna said firmly. "I'll not let you risk your life again on a fool's errand."

Then she remembered that a group had left for Fort Benton earlier that afternoon. If she left soon, she told Daniel, she could catch up to the men and have them bring the news that Daniel was safe. Daniel objected to Anna leaving alone in the near dark, but she insisted that he stay behind and busied herself getting ready to ride.

XVIII.

Anna rode hard and caught up with the group a few miles from the stage stop. They too worried about Anna being out alone but agreed to pass along the news of Daniel. As promised, the group went directly to the Antlers, where Anna had said they could find some of Daniel's friends. Upon their arrival at the saloon, they announced with gusto that they had news of Daniel. The buzz in the room quickly receded, and one of the travelers, a bit of a showman, stood on a chair and cleared his throat. "Daniel McHarg made it through the storm," the traveler reported. "He's still a little worse off for his night in the cold, but he's alive and resting up at the stage stop. He plans to return to Fort Benton tomorrow."

The men at the Antlers all knew Daniel, and they gleefully received the news as a better-than-usual excuse to drink too much. They competed for the right to buy the travelers their first drink, and a few celebratory toasts quickly followed. Opening the floor, John played it straight at first, with a simple appreciation for the fact that Daniel's luck had held, but soon slipped into a riff on Daniel's love of whiskey and poetry: "I'm not sure which of the two he loves most—they go hand in hand—but I do know that Nellie trumps them both. Here's to Daniel and Nellie. May they live long and raise a brood of little Daniels to help with those stinking cows!"

The toast was the reminder John needed to find Nellie and give her the news. He immediately headed for her aunt's house and saw Nellie sitting by the fireplace as he approached the front door. A light knock brought her to the door right away. She was relieved to see John's familiar grin, likely enhanced by the whiskey but not an expression he'd wear if he bore bad news.

John was perplexed by Nellie's reaction to his report. She seemed unable to accept the good news, probably because she had worried for too long and had imagined darker outcomes that had become set in her mind. It was as if she needed some proof, which John couldn't provide.

"Nellie, that's all I know," he said. "But I'll take you to the Antlers, and you can ask them yourself."

Nellie declined, but she got John to agree that they'd head out first thing the next morning and meet Daniel on the road.

Nellie spent another restless night but awoke with a sense of renewal and trust in the news about Daniel. John, Nellie, and a few other friends of Daniel made up the little party that set out to greet him that morning. They easily reached the high ground between Shonkin and Arrow Creeks. It was flat, open country where a rider could be seen at a great distance. Nellie watched the horizon closely and finally spotted a distant figure slowly making its way along the stage road. Some kind of device trailed behind his horse. Although there was no proof of the figure's identity, the group broke into a gallop and closed the distance quickly. They arrived breathless but assured by the recognition that the man's striped blanket coat, a gift from Jean Baptiste, could only belong to Daniel.

Meanwhile, Daniel was less aware of his surroundings. He rode slowly and remained deep in thought. He had spotted the group at some distance but had no idea who they might be. Thus, he was astonished to see that Nellie was among the group. Her frantic waving drew Daniel's attention, and her shouts of "Daniel!" were the final signs he needed to realize that he was almost home.

It was a tearful but sweet reunion. When he had held Nellie long enough while maintaining the proper dignity for the occasion, Daniel turned his attention to John and the others and thanked them for bringing Nellie along. "But you fellows certainly took your time," he joked. "Did the Antlers finally run out of whiskey, or are you all just out for a ride?"

In response, a few of the men dismounted and pelted Daniel with snow. Daniel joined the little fray and the sound of his laughter reassured Nellie that he'd be alright. John ended the little ruckus when he clamped Daniel in a bear hug and lugged him back to his horse.

XIX.

That spring, when the ground finally thawed, Daniel and Nellie buried Jean Baptiste on their property near the river amid a stand of cottonwood. Many of the old-timers, along with some of Daniel's friends, gathered for the service. News of Jean Baptiste's death had spread to the Blackfoot community, and Follows Bear stood silently as a priest uttered a traditional remembrance, consigning Jean Baptiste's soul to God and calling for the group to join him in prayer. After the priest finished, Follows Bear asked to be heard. At first he spoke in his native language, and then he switched to French, which Daniel translated for the group.

"Jean Baptiste was a different kind of white man," said Follows Bear. "He lived in both worlds and knew the wisdom of each. I pray the Great Spirit will be kind to his soul and bring us more of his kind."

After everyone left, Nellie and Daniel stood looking out at the range and the few head of cattle that had survived the winter.

"It was a hard winter, Daniel, and such a sad sight to behold. We have so few left," said Nellie.

Daniel, who seemed surprisingly happy given the occasion, had some news to share. "Well, that's about to change, Nellie. I just talked to a man this morning, someone who came to pay his respects to Jean Baptiste. He thinks we have the best land in the whole Teton Valley. He has some money to invest and wants to partner with us and build up a herd. I told him yes. Unless, of course, you object."

Nellie's response was a smile—the same smile Daniel remembered so well from that day on the Red Cloud.

'Twas the dear smile when naebody did mind us,
'Twas the bewitching, sweet, stown glance o' kindness.

The path before them now seemed clear.

End Note

This is a work of fiction. It was inspired by events in the life of Mell Keith, my great grandfather, who left New Brunswick, Canada in 1879 and went west, arriving in Fort Benton, Montana Territory in 1881. Mell and several other Keiths from the same small area in New Brunswick settled in Montana in the 1880's. Some of them prospered there while others, including Mell, never found their stride. Mell left Montana about 1890 and continued west to Spokane. Although the story is fictional, Mell did own property on the Teton River, spent some time in the mining camp at Maiden, and married a woman named Nellie Sage, who arrived in Montana aboard the Red Cloud accompanied by her mother and sister. Two of the newspaper quotes are authentic, though altered slightly, including the congratulatory piece on the wedding.

Tom Keith

Tom Keith has long had an interest in history and is the author of *A Few Days in August: A Story of Death and Survival in the Patwell Family during the Dakota Conflict of 1862*, an account of events in which several members of his family were participants. *When Everything Changed* is his first work of fiction. Tom is a principal in a planning and design firm and lives in Colorado.